D1385390

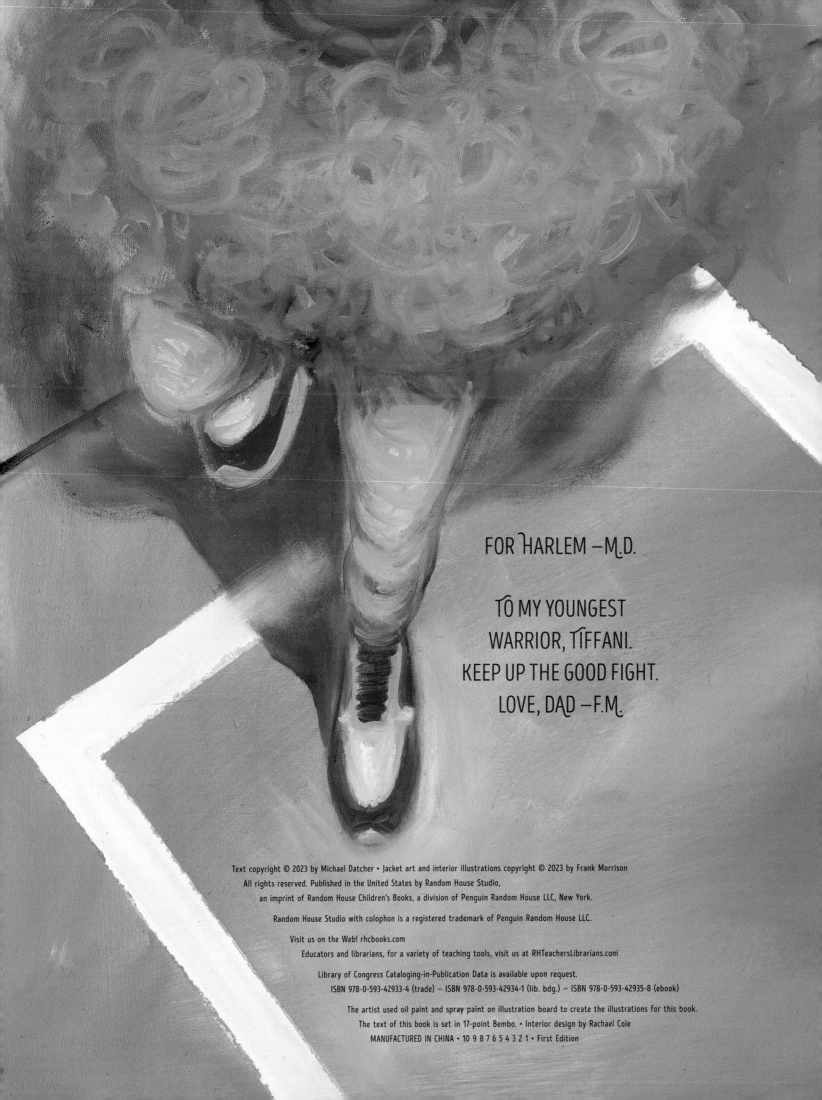

FOR HARLEM —M.D.

TO MY YOUNGEST
WARRIOR, TIFFANI.
KEEP UP THE GOOD FIGHT.
LOVE, DAD —F.M.

Text copyright © 2023 by Michael Datcher • Jacket art and interior illustrations copyright © 2023 by Frank Morrison
All rights reserved. Published in the United States by Random House Studio,
an imprint of Random House Children's Books, a division of Penguin Random House LLC, New York.

Random House Studio with colophon is a registered trademark of Penguin Random House LLC.

Visit us on the Web! rhcbooks.com
Educators and librarians, for a variety of teaching tools, visit us at RHTeachersLibrarians.com

Library of Congress Cataloging-in-Publication Data is available upon request.
ISBN 978-0-593-42933-4 (trade) — ISBN 978-0-593-42934-1 (lib. bdg.) — ISBN 978-0-593-42935-8 (ebook)

The artist used oil paint and spray paint on illustration board to create the illustrations for this book.
The text of this book is set in 17-point Bembo. • Interior design by Rachael Cole
MANUFACTURED IN CHINA • 10 9 8 7 6 5 4 3 2 1 • First Edition

HARLEM at FOUR

WRITTEN BY
DR. MICHAEL DATCHER

ILLUSTRATED BY
FRANK MORRISON

RANDOM HOUSE STUDIO NEW YORK

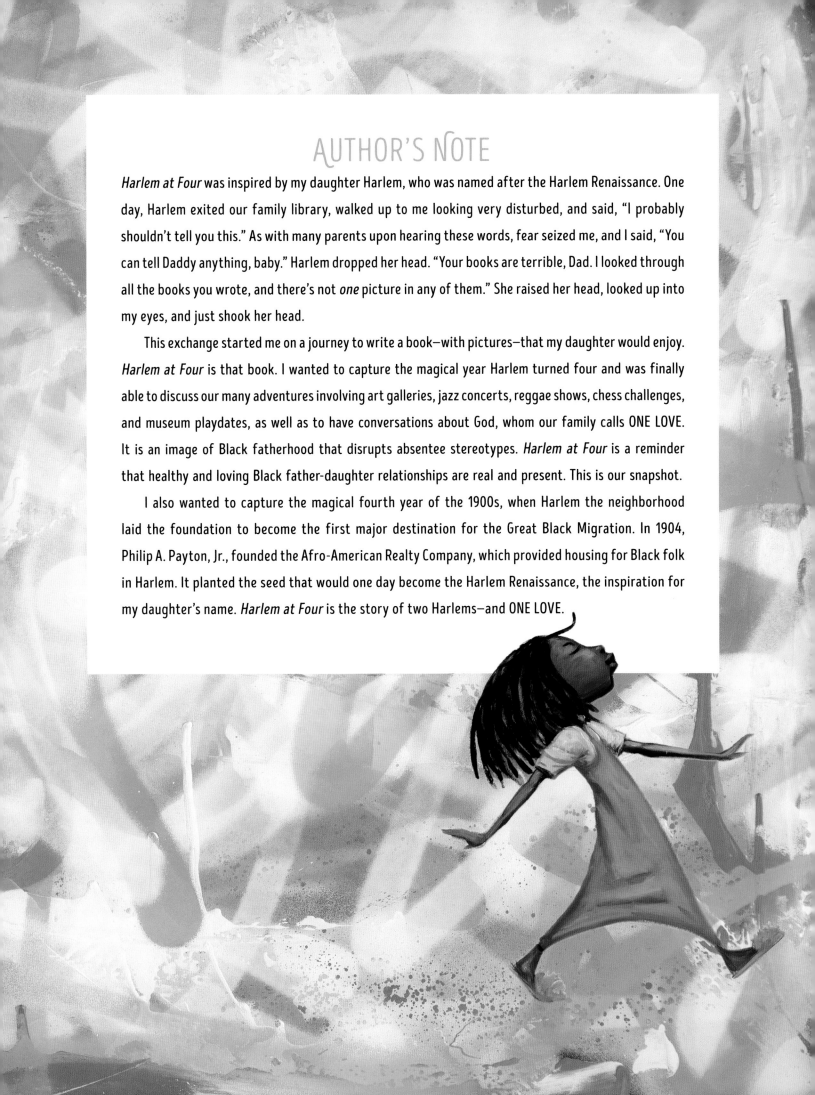

AUTHOR'S NOTE

Harlem at Four was inspired by my daughter Harlem, who was named after the Harlem Renaissance. One day, Harlem exited our family library, walked up to me looking very disturbed, and said, "I probably shouldn't tell you this." As with many parents upon hearing these words, fear seized me, and I said, "You can tell Daddy anything, baby." Harlem dropped her head. "Your books are terrible, Dad. I looked through all the books you wrote, and there's not *one* picture in any of them." She raised her head, looked up into my eyes, and just shook her head.

This exchange started me on a journey to write a book—with pictures—that my daughter would enjoy. *Harlem at Four* is that book. I wanted to capture the magical year Harlem turned four and was finally able to discuss our many adventures involving art galleries, jazz concerts, reggae shows, chess challenges, and museum playdates, as well as to have conversations about God, whom our family calls ONE LOVE. It is an image of Black fatherhood that disrupts absentee stereotypes. *Harlem at Four* is a reminder that healthy and loving Black father-daughter relationships are real and present. This is our snapshot.

I also wanted to capture the magical fourth year of the 1900s, when Harlem the neighborhood laid the foundation to become the first major destination for the Great Black Migration. In 1904, Philip A. Payton, Jr., founded the Afro-American Realty Company, which provided housing for Black folk in Harlem. It planted the seed that would one day become the Harlem Renaissance, the inspiration for my daughter's name. *Harlem at Four* is the story of two Harlems—and ONE LOVE.

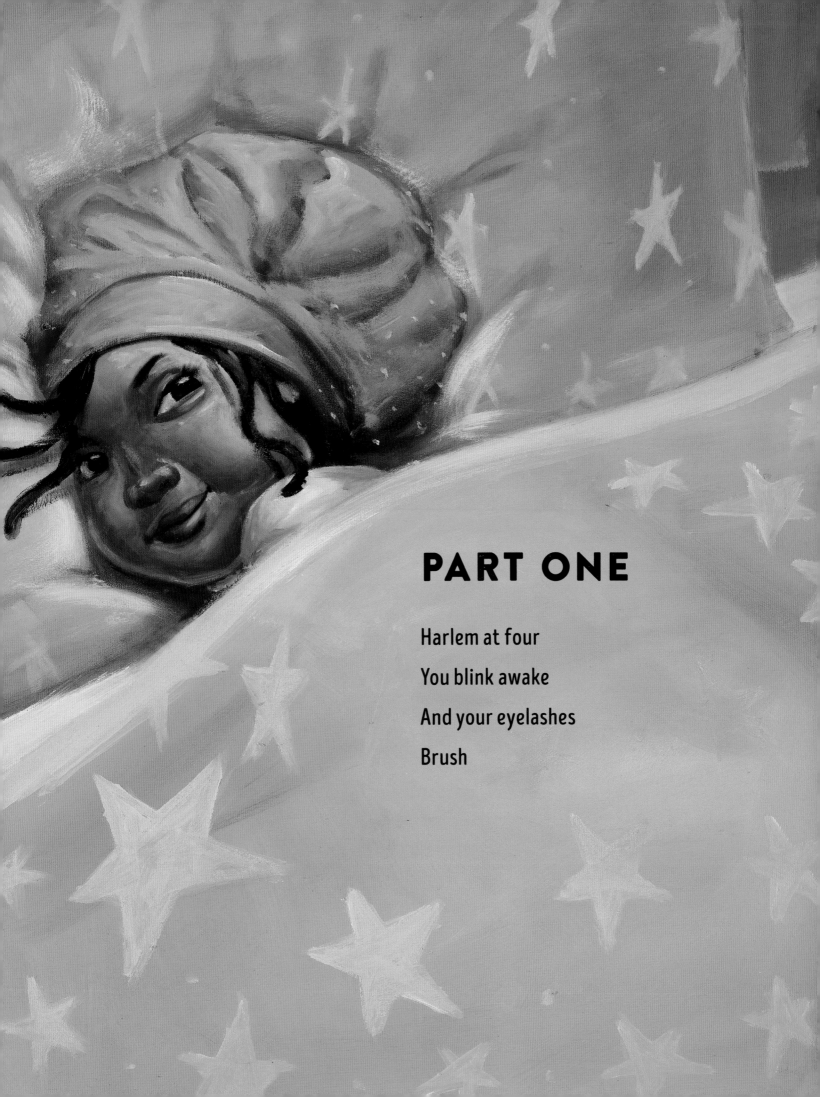

PART ONE

Harlem at four

You blink awake

And your eyelashes

Brush

A

Super Daddy "S"

Across my beating chest.

Sketch

Black Girl Magic

On my heart-shaped canvas.

Cameras can't capture

Your Malcolm X

Boulevard

Corner speaker confidence.

Fierce can't be photographed.

Shutter speed

Too slow

To frame you

Like the government
Sought to cage Black Panther
Afeni Shakur.

The jury said, "Not guilty"
Before
She gave birth
To Tupac Shakur
In Harlem.

Listening to
John Coltrane songs
Makes you sing
A Love Supreme.

THE JAZZ
IS FREE
BUT I DO TAKE TIPS

Cloudy days
Make you *Kind of Blue*
Like your favorite
Miles Davis record.

We bond on Black genius.

You take the A Train

Transformed into

My ride-share museum shoulders.

Rolling artsy

From Romare Bearden to Jean-Michel Basquiat.

Playdates with painters.

Before you take the A Train home.

Covered in watercolors

You awaken

At dawn

Praying to the sun

With reggae songs on your lips.

Singing *One Love*

And Bob Marley's

Three Little Birds

Who remind you that

Every little thing is gonna be all right.

Your pink pajamas

Match

Your pink protective goggles during

Harlem & Daddy's

Early-Morning Science Club.

The volcano erupts

Red lava on Valentine's Day!

You celebrate

Science experiment success

By playing your pink guitar.

Daddy keeps rhythm with a soul clap

In the background

While looking lovingly

At a Black girl
Named Harlem

With magical eyelashes
Painting a Super Daddy "S"
Across my beating chest.

PART TWO

In Harlem, New York's fourth year

Of the 20th century

The Father of Harlem

Philip A. Payton, Jr.

Became the proud parent of

The Afro-American Realty Company.

Papa Payton

Bought homes

In Harlem, the birthplace

Of author James Baldwin

Then rented them to

Brownstone-colored families

Because unfair white landlords
Blocked
Black moms and dads
From white blocks'
Brownstones.

That's not justice!

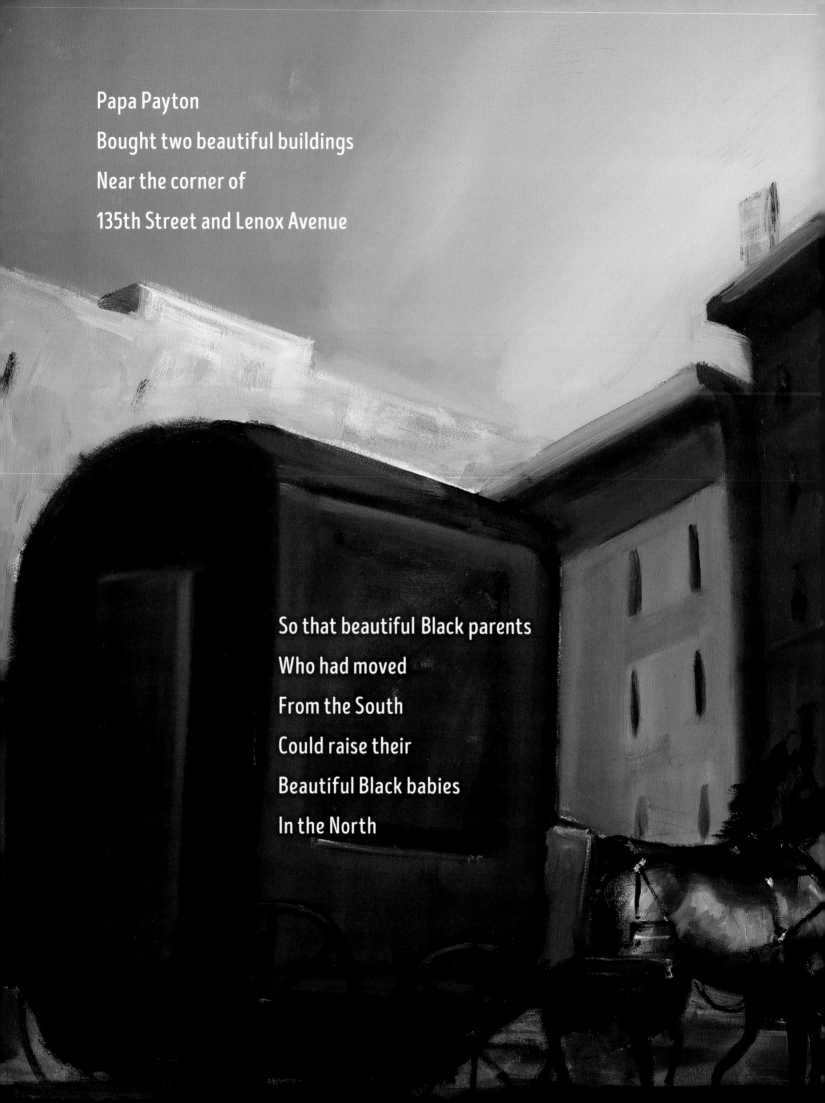

Papa Payton
Bought two beautiful buildings
Near the corner of
135th Street and Lenox Avenue

So that beautiful Black parents
Who had moved
From the South
Could raise their
Beautiful Black babies
In the North

As loving pioneers of
The Great Black Migration.

Black is beautiful.

In Harlem, New York's fourth year
Of the 20th century
New York City's
First subway line opened

On Lenox Avenue
And made a stop
On the corner
Of 135th Street and Lenox Avenue
So relatives could visit
Baby Black Roses
Growing up through concrete
In Papa Payton's buildings.

Years later

Harlem leaders

Decided to rename

Lenox Avenue

Malcolm X Boulevard

Because he was a Black Rose

Who preached justice

On the concrete corner

Of 135th and Lenox

To listening crowds,

Which included

A young social justice activist

And Street Corner Poet

Named Sonia Sanchez.

Malcolm X inspired Harlemites

To stand up for their rights

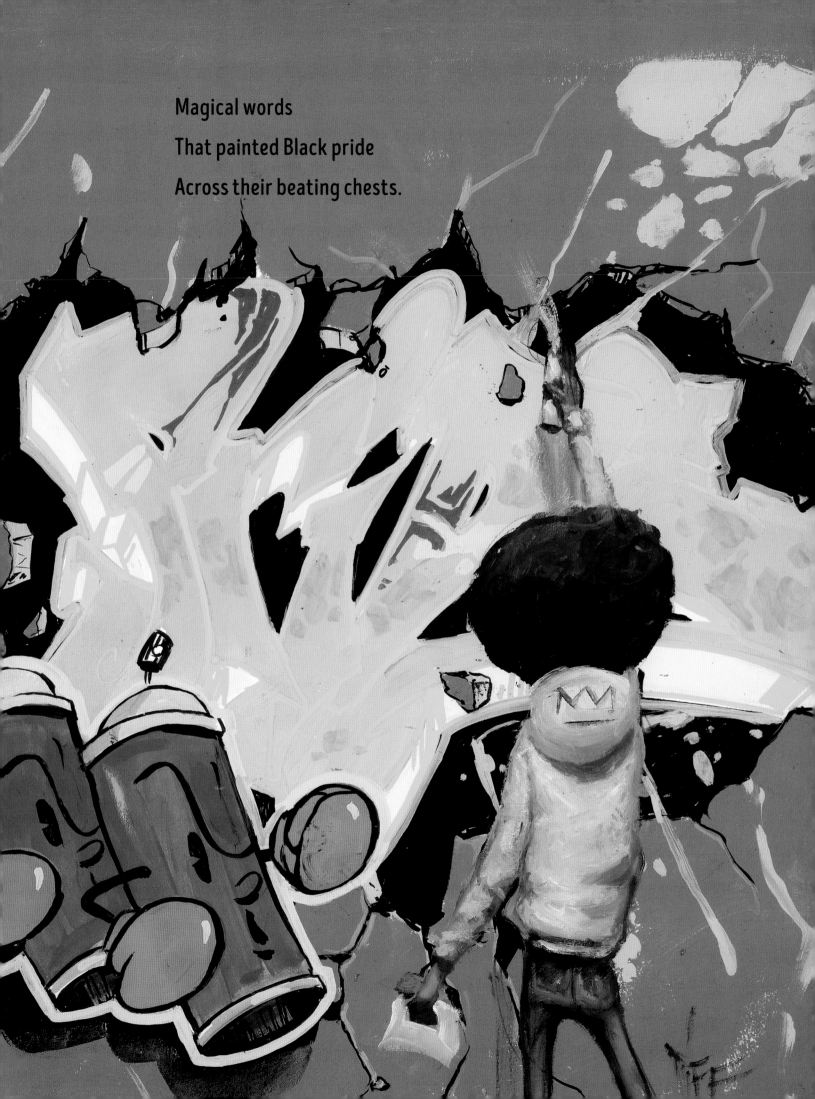

Magical words

That painted Black pride

Across their beating chests.

THE INCREDIBLE PEOPLE, PLACES, AND THINGS IN *HARLEM AT FOUR*

A TRAIN
A New York City subway line that travels through Harlem. The A Train was famously honored in the Duke Ellington Orchestra signature tune "Take the A Train," composed by Billy Strayhorn.

JAMES BALDWIN (1924-1987)
Born in Harlem, James Baldwin was a writer, intellectual, and civil rights activist. His essay collection *The Fire Next Time,* a seminal text in both African American literature and American race relations, argues that love is a crucial component of pushing forward the cause of social justice.

JEAN-MICHEL BASQUIAT (1960-1988)
A neo-Expressionist painter with roots in New York City's graffiti art, punk, and early hip-hop scenes, Basquiat created boldly colored paintings that often commented on politics and social issues. In 2017, his painting *Untitled* sold for a record-breaking $110.5 million.

ROMARE BEARDEN (1911-1988)
A member of the Harlem Artists Guild and a visual artist known for his innovative collages, Romare Bearden was one of the most acclaimed American artists of the 20th century. His work is displayed in many public art institutions, including the Metropolitan Museum of Art, the Whitney Museum of American Art, and the Studio Museum in Harlem—which he helped to establish.

BLACK GIRL MAGIC
Coined in 1999 by feminist author and scholar Dr. Joan Morgan, this phrase refers to a fierce quality of Black girls, which allows them to creatively and charismatically elevate above oppressive forces.

BROWNSTONES
Row houses whose bricks are covered with deep-brown sandstone, frequently carved with ornate designs. Brownstones are often found in Manhattan and Brooklyn.

JOHN COLTRANE (1926-1967)
An ambitiously innovative jazz saxophonist who rose to fame in trumpeter Miles Davis's First Great Quintet, John Coltrane was one of the most influential musicians in American history. After he left Davis and embarked on a spiritual journey through jazz, his John Coltrane Quartet recorded an album recognized as one of the greatest jazz records of all time: *A Love Supreme.*

MILES DAVIS (1926-1991)
Born in Alton, Illinois, and raised in nearby East St. Louis, jazz trumpeter Miles Davis was one of the most innovative and influential musicians in American history. Along with helping to define major jazz movements like bebop, cool jazz, and jazz fusion, Davis was an iconic cultural figure who symbolized Black pride, Black cool, and Black excellence.

THE GREAT BLACK MIGRATION
Frustrated with racial violence, social discrimination, and limited economic opportunities in the American South, Blacks began to move north in waves around 1910. By 1970, over six million African Americans had migrated north from the South, making the Great Black Migration one of the largest movements of people in American history.

HARLEM
The Manhattan neighborhood above Central Park, originally incorporated in 1660. Enhanced by the Great Black Migration, which began in the 1910s, Harlem birthed a cultural, political, and artistic flowering of Black excellence known as the Harlem Renaissance. It included the Black luminaries W. E. B. Du Bois, Zora Neale Hurston, Langston Hughes, and Josephine Baker.

KIND OF BLUE
This legendary 1959 album by the Miles Davis Quintet is the bestselling jazz album of all time. It is considered one of the greatest jazz records in history—and it features John Coltrane on tenor saxophone.

A LOVE SUPREME
A 1965 jazz album by saxophonist John Coltrane, widely considered a masterpiece. The four parts of his suite about spirituality include "Acknowledgement," "Resolution," "Pursuance," and "Psalm."

BOB MARLEY (1945–1981)

A musician from Kingston, Jamaica, who was a creator and leading proponent of the Jamaican folk music known as reggae. His music's mixture of spirituality, social commentary, and Black pride made Marley one of the most respected and beloved figures in the global music community.

"ONE LOVE"

This iconic reggae song by Bob Marley and the Wailers is on their 1977 album *Exodus.* The song suggests that justice, spirituality, and love must be present for there to be unity among people.

PHILIP A. PAYTON, JR. (1876–1917)

Philip A. Payton, Jr., was an entrepreneur who founded the Afro-American Realty Company in 1904. Payton managed and bought residential properties, primarily on Harlem blocks formerly forbidden to Blacks—and opened their doors to Black residents. Payton came to be known as the Father of Harlem because he laid the foundation for Harlem's status as the first major northern destination during the Great Black Migration.

SONIA SANCHEZ (b. 1934)

Sonia Sanchez is a poet, educator, and human rights activist. Born in Birmingham, Alabama, Sanchez moved to Harlem as a child and became an influential figure in the civil rights movement. Her collection *Homegirls and Handgrenades* won an American Book Award and is widely considered a classic text in African American poetry.

AFENI SHAKUR (1947–2016)

A political activist and a Harlem chapter leader of the influential Black Panther Party, a Black nationalist human rights group, Afeni Shakur famously represented herself during the Panther 21 trial. She helped win acquittals for all twenty-one Black Panthers who were facing conspiracy charges. Her Harlem-born son, Tupac Shakur, was one of the most iconic artists in the history of hip-hop.

TUPAC SHAKUR (1971–1996)

Hip-hop artist, poet, and social activist Tupac Shakur's mixture of Black consciousness, fierce rebelliousness, and rough urban poetics made him one of hip-hop's most famous icons.

SPEAKERS' CORNER

Since the 1910s, orators (often standing on wooden soapboxes) have given speeches about politics and social issues at this famous Harlem street corner, at Malcolm X Boulevard and 135th Street. Marcus Garvey—a Jamaican-born activist, community organizer, and proponent of Black uplift—gave his first American speech here in 1916. In 1987, Lenox Avenue was co-named Malcolm X Boulevard to honor its new namesake, who was a frequent corner speaker.

STUDIO MUSEUM IN HARLEM

Founded in 1968, this Harlem museum focuses on artists of African descent. Its permanent collection has over nine thousand works, including the art of Romare Bearden, Elizabeth Catlett, Jacob Lawrence, and Betye Saar.

"THREE LITTLE BIRDS"

One of reggae legend Bob Marley's most famous recordings, "Three Little Birds" is on the 1977 album *Exodus.* The song is more popularly known by its uplifting refrain: "Don't worry about a thing, 'cause every little thing is gonna be all right."

MALCOLM X (1925–1965)

Malcolm X was a human rights activist and outspoken proponent of Black self-determination. During the civil rights movement, he rose to prominence as lead minister of Harlem's Nation of Islam Mosque No. 7 while also serving as national spokesman for this Black nationalist organization.

SELECTED SOURCES

Gill, Jonathan. *Harlem: The Four Hundred Year History from Dutch Village to Capital of Black America.* New York: Grove Press, 2011.

Lewis, David Levering. *When Harlem Was in Vogue.* New York: Penguin Books, 1981.

McGruder, Kevin. *Philip Payton: The Father of Black Harlem.* New York: Columbia University Press, 2021.

Payne, Les, and Tamara Payne. *The Dead Are Arising: The Life of Malcolm X.* New York: Liveright, 2020.

Zimroth, Peter L. *Perversions of Justice: The Prosecution and Acquittal of the Panther 21.* New York: Viking, 1974.